Rooster Tells a Tale

by Winston White
illustrated by Randall Enos

Barksbee
BOOKS

SILVER BURDETT & GINN

Dusk settled over the farm. All the animals gathered outside the barn to hear Rooster's tale of the day.

Rooster cleared his throat. "Tonight, my friends, I will tell you the story of the fox and the crow. This is a story which has been told many . . ."

"Rooster," piped up Hen. "Must you tell a story about a fox? As you know, Fox is my natural enemy. I would rather not hear a story about a fox and a crow."

"All right, then," said Rooster. "Instead of the fox and the crow, I will tell you about the pig and the crow. One day . . ."

"Just a minute, Rooster," interrupted
   Pig. "Must you tell a story about a pig?
   As you know, we pigs are always said
   to be dirty, lazy creatures. I would
   rather not hear a story about a pig and
   a crow."

"Whatever you say," said Rooster.
"Then I will tell you about the cow and
   the crow. One day . . ."

"Stop right there," said Cow. "Must you tell a story about a cow? As you know, we cows are quiet animals who mind our own business. I would rather not hear a story about a cow and a crow."

"If it really bothers you," said Rooster, "I'll tell my tale about the horse and the crow. Once long ago . . ."

"Hold your horses," said Horse.
"Must you tell a story about a horse?
As you know, we horses are seen as
flighty, fidgety animals. I would
rather not hear a story about a horse
and a crow."

"Fine, fine," said Rooster. "Then I
must tell this story about the rooster
and the crow."

"Once a rooster met a crow," began Rooster. "The crow had a fine piece of cheese in her beak which the rooster wanted. The rooster began to tell the crow how pretty her voice must be since she was such a beautiful bird.

"Finally the crow was so pleased by the rooster's words that she opened her beak to sing. The cheese fell out and the rooster ran off with it."

"And so," ended Rooster, "you can see what a smart, clever fellow the rooster was."

And with that, all the animals spoke at once.

"It should have been the hen and
  the crow," said Hen.
"It should have been the pig and
  the crow," said Pig.
"It should have been the cow and
  the crow," said Cow.
"It should have been the horse and
  the crow," said Horse.

"But it was the rooster and the
  crow," said Rooster, pleased with
  himself.

Just then a beautiful black crow with
a piece of cheese in her beak flew into
a tree near the barn.

Here's my chance, thought Hen and
Pig and Cow and Horse.

"Please give me that cheese," said Hen.
"I'd like to hear you sing," said Pig.
"I'm very hungry tonight," said Cow.
"Won't you drop that cheese?"
asked Horse.

Fox crept into the barnyard and began to praise the crow. "My, Crow, you must have a beautiful voice to match your beautiful feathers.

"In fact, you must have the most beautiful voice in the world. If only all these animals could hear you sing."

Crow was so pleased to hear all
these compliments from Fox that she
opened her beak and let out a caw.
But she also let out the cheese and
Fox scooped it up and ran off into
the dusk.

All the animals agreed that Rooster's
story had been right in the first place.